72 Hours

E. M. McConnell

Other Books By The Author

The Dust Collector
The Sunset Sovereign
Of Swans and Stars
Love Lost and Found
PTSD Is a 4 Letter Word
Cinquains
Haiku
Death by Sugar

This book is dedicated to all the women who were confined to asylums in the 19th century for postnatal depression, hysteria, or simply on the say so of their husbands.

A casual stroll through the lunatic asylum shows that
faith does not prove anything.
Nietzsche

Contents

Chapter 1
Day 1

The car door slammed shut behind her with a satis-
fying thud. She did not look back. Her eyes were on
her prize, the next step in her career. She let out a
breath, and smoothed down her suit. She had been
asking for this visit for months, in order to finalise her
research. This building had a past, and she intended
to show it to the world. Her eyes roved over the clean,
well kept building, and the red brick front wrapped in
dark ivy. From this particular entrance, it did not look
like a secure hospital. With the gravel at the front and
the neat potted plants, it could even be a hotel, or a
retreat. It looked calm, orderly, and safe.

The sign gleamed carefully at the side of the large
double doors. Rivers Asylum, 1914-1980. They didn't
call it an asylum nowadays of course, as there were
better words for it, but this was the original name and
so they kept the plaque there as a memorial of sorts.
Nowadays it was called Rivers Hospital.

The door opened and a man stepped out, buttoning his plain grey jacket as he went. He was of average height, with wire-framed glasses and slightly thinning hair. His paunch told her that he preferred to sit at a desk than be active. But his eyes were keen and his smile was friendly, as he walked over, holding his hand out for her to shake.

"Dr. Carter? Dr. Rebecca Carter?"

"Yes, that's me. I'm Dr. Carter. And you are?"

He shook her hand, firmly, once, before stepping back. "My name is Benson. I'm not a doctor, I just handle the administrative side. I suppose you're expecting to meet the team? They're just finishing up the debrief and then will be able to see you. Can I escort you in and organise your necessaries?"

His manner was cordial, almost debonair, as he stepped effortlessly into his role. She assented, taking her bags and walking alongside him towards the aged building.

As they entered, the atmosphere changed. The interior was clean and orderly, much like the exterior, but there was an undeniable sense of history lingering in the air. It was as if the past was overlaid with the present, waiting, watching.

There were transparent lockers to the right of the large receptionist desk, with a sign ordering all visitors to leave their phones, food and money behind. Benson waited politely as she complied, taking her purse and phone out, and retrieving the large key with a plastic fob. No. 32 was emblazoned on the front. Her own age. That was an omen if anything was.

Rebecca examined the interior, wondering how different it would have been then as the asylum. Would it have been busy in this part? Would they, too, have decorated the entryway with green plants and comfortable chairs?

Benson cleared his throat, eager to get on his way.

"I'm looking forward to meeting the team," Dr. Carter said, her voice steady. She wondered if he could hear her inner excitement. "Thank you for approving this visit, Mr. Benson. I've been eager to explore River's archives and learn more about its role in the psychiatric history of the region."

Benson nodded appreciatively and led her down a long hallway lined with photographs of the hospital's past, doctors and staff who had worked there, and various events that had taken place over the years. The more recent photographs were in colour, but some were black and white, with solemn faces. In each, the building loomed behind them, the structure that housed them all, ill and well alike.

As they walked, Benson waved to the pictures. "We take great pride in preserving the history of this institution. It played a significant role in psychiatric care during its time, and we believe it's important to acknowledge its impact, both positive and negative, on mental health treatment."

Dr. Carter listened attentively, wondering how much he knew of the history of this particular institution. Was he aware of its dark past, or was he referring to the darker history of psychiatric care in general?

Arriving at a small conference room, Benson gestured for her to take a seat. "The team will be with you shortly," he said with a warm smile. "If there's anything you need in the meantime, don't hesitate to ask. I will get your ID ready so you can access the buildings and will return to do your tour when you have finished up here if one of your colleagues doesn't volunteer. You're staying for three days, is that right?"

"That's right. I've got limited time before I present my research findings to the university and my publisher, but I think that three days is more than enough. I only need to access the archives, interview some patients and the staff, and then I can be on my way."

He smiled. "Well it's great to have you here. We do have quarters for the residential staff so we can house you there while you are here. That makes it easier than having to sign you in and out all the time. Unless you would prefer a hotel?"

"No, no," she replied hastily. "The residential quarters are just fine. Thank you, Mr Benson."

He bowed slightly and left, closing the door quietly behind him. Rebecca's eyes scanned the room, taking in the old-fashioned décor that hinted at the room's past use while maintaining its functionality as a modern workspace. The wooden walls were filled with more photographs, most of which were familiar to her. One caught her eye, a black and white photo with a man standing in front of the building. He was dressed in a suit and of course looked more serious than death. She peered at the caption but couldn't read it. The writing was too faded. She resolved to ask the team when they arrived.

The door opened quietly, ushering in a young woman with neat hair and glasses. She smiled, hunching her shoulders slightly, as she tiptoed into the room and settled herself into a chair. She looked as if she wanted the chair to swallow her up. "I'm the first. That will never do! Hello, I'm Natalie. I'm new here. And you're Dr. Carter?"

Rebecca smiled, walking over to shake her hand. "I am. Thanks so much for seeing me. I'm spending the next three days here to do some research on the old hospital, take some interviews from patients, and from staff, of course."

Natalie's eyes were wide. "Which patients were you planning to see?"

"Well, I am sure Benson, or yourselves, can give me a list of those who are lucid enough to be interviewed and are happy to talk."

A flicker of relief crossed her face, then disappeared. Rebecca wondered at it. Who did she think she meant? Rebecca sat down in the adjacent chair, leaving her briefcase on the table. "Where were you here before Rivers? And are you enjoying it?"

Natalie's face lit up and she pushed her glasses up on her face. "Oh, I am enjoying it, although there is a lot to remember with security and protocols and such like. I'm always worried about doing something wrong! I came straight from university, this is my first proper job. I want to get some experience here and then maybe go into something therapeutic, qualify, you know."

Rebecca did know. It had taken her many years to get to the position she had, and now, with the final elements of research in her reach, she was finally about to achieve it. All her years of hard work would bring recognition. She would be the leading expert on asylums. She started, not realising that Natalie had continued speaking.

"What is your research about, specifically?"

Rebecca resisted the urge to get her papers out and launch into a full-blown presentation. "It's about the history and development of psychiatric care, really, but I don't want to go into specifics till the others arrive. Do you know if they are coming?"

"Oh I am sure they will be. Perhaps they got caught up with paperwork. But we are very keen to have you here, Dr Carter!"

She was sure they were. But they were taking up her precious time by not being here, and she did not need that. Natalie sat back again, subdued, and they sat in an awkward silence. Rebecca could hear a clock ticking somewhere, one of those ponderous slow ticks that could only be a grandfather clock.

The door opened at last, and three more people came in, all smiling and apologising as they entered. The first, a sandy-haired man with a checked shirt and his ID card prominently displayed on his chest, made the introductions.

"We got delayed, I am so sorry, Dr Carter. Sometimes the staff like to make everyone wait just to be sure, they are very risk averse, you know. Everything has to be counted in and out. My name is Dr Julian Smetham, I'm the person who oversees the care of our residents, and this is my colleague Laura Tweed, who heads up the Education Department. She has really modernised our education programme and has brought such meaning to our patients. I know you will be keen to talk with her."

Laura leaned forward, shaking her hand with a solid, firm, handshake. She, too, was dressed smartly, in a trouser suit and her ID attached at her waist. Beneath the jacket, Rebecca could see a belt and a small device attached to it.

The last person was a man, dressed in a pale green uniform and white shoes. He was dark-haired, bearded, with friendly eyes. He twinkled at her as he leaned to shake her hand. "I'm Adam. I'm just a nurse here!"

Dr Julian guffawed. "Just a nurse! Such modesty, Adam." He turned back to Rebecca, his smile widening. "So here you have us, your team for the next three days. We are at your disposal, where we can, of course, to give you the information that you need, escort you about and generally keep you safe. As you are a civilian visitor, we have a responsibility to ensure that your stay here is pleasant and smooth sailing."

A civilian visitor. That was code for, you may have qualifications but you are not one of us. She could live with it. They did not possess the knowledge that she needed anyway, the real information should be in those archives. But she smiled and nodded, anyway. These were her colleagues, and they could other her as much as they wanted.

"I will need access to the archives, of course, and will be interviewing some patients as well as staff to finish off my research. Would you be able to give me a list of patients who are willing to be interviewed? And will I need to be escorted, being civilian personnel?" She smiled as she spoke, watching the point strike home. This was her three days, and she would get the research that she needed. Dr Julian took the point and nodded briskly. "I have a file for you of patients and their usual schedules. You will have full access to the archives, of course, and Adam here has graciously agreed to escort you. Isn't that right, Adam?"

Adam rose a little from the spot that he had taken perched on the table, arms crossed. "That's correct, yes, yes. If you don't mind, of course."

"I don't mind. Do I need one of those while I'm here?" She pointed to the alarm that nestled into his trousers, tucking itself under his stomach. His hands went to it reflexively, touching it twice before withdrawing his hands.

"Oh, the alarm? No, you're not here long enough for one of those. You'll have your ID which has your face programmed into it, and the staff can buzz you in and out on that. If there are any problems, not that there will be of course," he laughed nervously, "then I am here to handle it. You're not going to be around the patients that much, are you?"

There was that flicker of hesitance again, as if they didn't want her around the patients all that much. She logged it to think about later. There was something that they were keeping to themselves, certainly. She watched him for a moment, seeing his reaction to her scrutiny. Adam fidgeted a little.

"Not all that much, no. It depends on what they want to say, of course."

Laura rose from her seat, adjusting her jacket. "I have classes to be getting on with, Rebecca, it's been a pleasure. Do come and see me when you have time and have a tour of the Department. Alright?" Laura exchanged a glance with Dr Julian as she left, her heels clacking on the floor. The Doctor then cleared his throat. "Well I had best be getting on with things too, I am sure. There's no rest for the wicked, and all that!" His laugh was a bray, shooting out of his mouth quickly, landing in the awkward silence.

"If you need me, Dr Carter, Adam knows where to find me. I'm sure you're itching to get to it!" Turning on his heel, he left, leaving the two of them alone.

Adam clapped his hands together. "Well, let's get you started then. Benson should have your ID, and I can take you for a short tour of the facility before dropping you off in the archives. How does that sound?"

"That's fine. What about my things?"

"Oh you can leave them here for now, they're perfectly safe. Shall we?"

He gestured for her to follow, holding the door open. She followed, feeling that bubble of excitement rising again. *This was it, at last. Rebecca, you will find the secrets of River Hospital, and make a name for yourself at last. At last.*

As she left the boardroom, she felt as if she were crossing a threshold into the unknown. She smiled. At last.

Chapter 2

Adam was certainly an organised tour guide. He marched them both to pick up Rebecca's ID, which was a plain white plastic card that was threaded onto a chain. The orderly assured her that her image was programmed into the card itself and that they had matched the card with her face. She touched it again, to be sure it was there.

The outer part of the facility was mainly corridors with glass windows opening onto a pleasant garden, the walls lined with neat office doors and modest name plates. They reached the reception again, turning inward. Rebecca felt jangled by the security process, of handing her briefcase over, of being searched thoroughly by an expressionless woman dressed in white.

Stepping through the doors into the hospital felt like crossing into a different world. It was quieter, muffled. A sense of watchfulness gnawed at her, as if something lurked in the shadows. The linoleum flooring swallowed up their steps, cushioning the sound. The walls were still white, but the lights were dim, causing sickly green shadows to climb the walls. Rebecca shivered. Adam didn't seem to notice, as he continued his refrain.

"We have 284 beds available in the hospital but currently we have around 180 patients. We have a mix of female and male patients, but of course they are housed separately. Every day the patients have therapeutic time, which includes Education, talking Therapy, and some fresh air in the gardens. Medications are administered promptly at 10 and at 5pm, just after the evening meal. Lights out are at 9, but that doesn't affect you as you are in staff quarters. I will show you one of the female wards, we can pass by the Education Building too, as that's near the entrance to the Archives. The Archives are underground, you know. It preserves all the documents better."

She didn't know. But she nodded politely, just in case he wanted an affirmation. But he did not look at her, striding along, his eyes focused, with none of the amused twinkle he had before. Here, in these corridors, he was not just a nurse. She wondered if he enjoyed having the ability to move around freely, while his charges were contained.

The corridor continued, narrowing, as if they were stepping into a green pipe, being flushed towards something, pushed away. She felt the current slip under her feet, the rushing sound in her ears. She shook her head slightly, focusing.

No, she still heard the rushing sound. It was almost as if she could hear voices, just out of focus, a whispering from another room.

Her blood cooled as fear took hold. What could she hear? Adam was talking, his mouth moving as he looked back and forth, but she could not hear him. The whisper scratched inside her brain, trying to climb in, to claim a space.

Her hand tightened on her briefcase, digging her nails in. The sensation brought her focus with a snap. She blinked twice, forcing herself to focus.

"And how many women do you have here currently?"

Adam blinked owlishly at her for a moment. "We do not have as many, as most go to the female only suite in the north of the country. Some prefer it here, and it is quieter. I think we have twenty or thirty long-term female patients. Occasionally we get visitors, those who need specialist assessment or a visit from relatives locally or something. Ah, here we are."

He turned, pausing with a flourish at a set of double doors with no handle and no visible lock. There were small windows in the doors, rectangular strips of reinforced glass. Adam looked up towards the black device in the corner of the door. Nothing happened.

"Come stand by me," he muttered. "They need to see your face, too."

She moved forward, facing a camera, wondering who it was behind the winking red light, and if they ever looked closely at who went in. The doors hissed, and Adam pushed at the door, letting it open away from them in a smooth action. She stepped onto the ward.

It was a big room. There were windows at the end, if you could call them windows when they did not open and were reinforced with mesh on the outside. They might not live behind bars, but they were not going to taste freedom anytime soon.

The room itself was set out in an organised fashion, with the corner at the left filled with hospital issue armchairs surrounding a quietly burbling television, and the rest of the room taken up with trestle tables set up with various activities. Rebecca noticed art supplies, embroidery and even a potter's wheel which was sitting unnoticed, gathering dust. There was a small enclosed room with a sink, chairs and a kettle, and a few cups stacked neatly beside cheerful cannisters probably containing hospital issue coffee and tea.

At the far end, to the right, there was a nurse station with a room behind. There was nobody at the station, and the door behind it was closed. Rebecca looked around for staff, seeing a small group of people working together on something at a table in the corner and one dark haired girl sitting on her own with a book. She examined the group at the table more closely, recognising a green uniform at last.

"There does not seem to be many patients," she whispered to Adam. "I see only five?"

He frowned. "Yes, that is a little disappointing. Perhaps they are at therapy or been called away for something. There are the bedrooms, of course, just behind the brew room, but we are not encouraged to go in there. Well," he hesitated. "I can, as I am staff, but -"

"It isn't appropriate for me, yes," Rebecca responded, perhaps a little stiffly. She was getting tired of being othered in this place already.

He shot her a quick, relieved, smile. "Perhaps you would like to talk to the patients for a moment, and I will go and check if there is anything happening today?"

She nodded, watching him scuttle off with interest. Perhaps he was involved with one of the staff. It happened a lot in environments like this. Looking around at the plain walls and the cold, unyielding chairs, she could see why. The girl with a book had not moved. Taking the opportunity, she walked over, smiling, her hand out at the ready. The girl did not seem to notice, her eyes staring past the book resting limply in her hands. The book was upside down.

"Hello, hello, can you hear me?"

She walked closer, assessing the patient. She was young, her hair long and a little matted at the back. Her hands were thin, and she had dirt under her long fingernails. She was still staring, her face in repose, her eyes distant. Rebecca paused, wondering if she should speak to another, perhaps one of those who were sitting at the table, rather than this one. Perhaps she had just been given her medication.

As she stopped, about to turn away, the girl's head snapped towards her, her eyes dark, alert. Her lips moved, whispering something that Rebecca could not hear. Rebecca took a step back, just out of reach of the girl. Just in case. After all, Adam was somewhere else, and she had not been given a handy alarm device. Was she even supposed to be on her own?

The girl had stopped whispering but was still staring.

Rebecca smiled awkwardly, forcing her mouth to move. "I'm sorry to disturb you. My name is Dr Carter, I am conducting research in the hospital. Shall I leave you to your, er, book?"

The girl continued to stare, her face slack, her forehead beginning to furrow. The life returned to her suddenly, as awareness poured into her eyes.

"Oh, hello, Doctor. Are you here to fix me?"

Rebecca shifted her feet, getting a comfortable position. "I am afraid I am just here in a research capacity. What is your name?"

"What would you like it to be?" The girl's eyes were hollow, her face calculating. Rebecca took another half step backwards.

"I don't need to know your name. I was being friendly. If you don't wish to give it, that is your right."

Rebecca's voice came out stiffly, from frozen lips. She cursed her words as she spoke them, knowing she was showing weakness, that she looked weak. But she could not take the words back as they swam towards the patient, climbing into her mind. The patient blinked slowly in a lizard-like fashion.

"Annie. I'm Annie, and I'm twenty. Does that rhyme? Do you rhyme, Dr Carter?"

This was wasting time. She nodded politely and stepped back again, looking to see if her escort had emerged yet.

"What did you want to ask me, Dr Carter?"

The patient was insistent. Inwardly she sighed even as she smiled a thin smile, determined not to fidget. "I am conducting research into how this hospital has evolved since its beginnings as an asylum. Are you treated well here, Annie?"

The girl began to hum, and rock slightly. Rebecca waited. She could be patient, and Matthew wasn't back, anyway. It wasn't like she could use the research beyond a brief comment in her paper. If the patient was that far gone, it wouldn't count what she thought. But that tune was familiar somehow. She waited, listening.

"They treat me well here, Dr Carter. Do not fear. They treat me well here."

Her eyes went back to the wall, her eyes assessing, moving up and down. Rebecca's eyes flicked nervously to the wall. There was nothing there. Should she call someone? But who to call? Adam, damn him, was still not back. Surely this was a duty of care? She would call someone.

Annie's eyes locked back on hers. "They treat me well. But I do not like the shadows. Don't go to the shadows, Dr Carter. They come at night. Don't go to them. They want you. You hear me? THEY WANT YOU!"

Her shout rang out of her mouth, landing squarely at her feet. Rebecca gasped, jumping back. Annie just returned to her book, eyes staring at text that was upside down, humming that damn song.

Rebecca had had enough. She squared her jaw, ignoring her fear, and marched back to where Adam had disappeared. There was nobody there, just a corridor threaded in that sickly green, and silence. She took a deep breath. *March down there, and find someone to escort you to Archives. Just do it!*

As her brain resolved to just do it, Adam at last appeared, chummily close to a nurse in similar clothing, a smile, and very fashionable glasses. He looked up, surprised, his attention sharpening.

"Oh, Rebecca, is everything alright? You look a little... worried."

Rebecca focused her gaze on Adam, ignoring the stifled giggle from the nurse. "I'm just eager to get to the Archives, Adam. If you're busy, perhaps you can find someone else to escort me?"

He got the point. Stepping away from the still snickering nurse, he straightened, his expression sobering. "No, not at all, Dr Carter. Did you get to speak to anyone on the ward?"

Don't go to the shadows, Dr Carter

"I spoke to one person, but I don't know if they will be able to sign a clearance form. Are the Archives far from here?"

It was a pointless question, really, but it served as a reminder of what he was there to do. He knew it, and he took the point as he nodded hastily to the nurse and escorted her out, not looking back at the expanse of tables and wide windows, and glass doors that were reinforced with mesh to keep them in. Rebecca looked. It was a prettier cage than some of the first patients that came here but it still was an incarceration. Three days till she could forget this place. Three days till she had proved her research, made her name, and could begin her career. 3 days.

Chapter 3

Chapter 4

Night fell, and Rebecca watched the moon rise from her small room in the grounds of the hospital. It was a comfortable room with all the facilities she needed, but sleep eluded her. The shadows whispered her name, and she was afraid. Clutching the quilt tightly under her chin, she screwed up her eyes and began to whisper a prayer, over and over again.

The room darkened as the moon disappeared behind clouds, and the shadows began to move, drawing closer and closer to the bed. One shadow stepped from the wall, humming a tune. They stepped near to the bed, and knelt down, examining Rebecca's face. The shadow, which had now taken on the distinct shape of a girl, smiled.

"Dr Carter, can you hear me? I've been looking for you. Can you hear me?"

The whisper came just next to her ear, teasing gently against her skin. She batted the interruption away, then turned towards it, opening her eyes. A young woman was kneeling in front of her. She was small, with long dark straight hair and dark eyes. Her white dress was plain and old-fashioned, covering her arms and her body up to her neck. Her eyes were a little sunken, with hollows under her eyes. Her lips smiled and she spoke again. "Dr Carter. Did I wake you? I've been looking for you."

Her voice was high, almost child-like. Rebecca wondered who she was. "You did wake me. How, how did you get in here?"

She propped herself up, looking around. She was not in her own room, neither at home nor in the guest suite that she had gone to just that evening.

This was somewhere else.

She looked around, taking in her surroundings, trying not to panic.. The beds were narrow, and plain, spanning the entire room. The wooden floor was polished and the walls were white. There were no paintings on the walls, just a sad looking Christ on a dark wood crucifix hanging by the door. The door was pale green, and shut. She did not recognise this place.

"Who are you? Where am I?"

The woman smiled again, showing gaps in her teeth. "Dr Carter, you're here with us. We called you. Don't you recognise me? I'm Jenny. I've been looking for you, Dr Carter. Do you recognise me?"

Rebecca struggled to sit upright, noticing her dress was also of the same style as the one Jenny was wearing. She plucked at it, feeling the fabric. "I don't know a Jenny. Who are you?"

"Don't be afraid, Dr Carter. We don't want to hurt you. We still live here, you see? We wanted to talk to you. I've been looking for you. Do you recognise me?"

Jenny. Jenny. The only Jenny she knew of was the one she had written down on the notebook just that day.

She looked back at her, feeling cold. "You wanted to talk to me, Jenny? Why?"

"Because you're a doctor, aren't you? I've never seen a lady doctor before. We're still here, you see. In the walls. I've been watching you. And you called me, Dr Carter. You called me out of the walls. And now I'm here. Don't you remember me?"

Rebecca spoke slowly, her lips numb. "I remember you, Jenny. You were sent to Rivers to be treated for melancholy. Is that right?"

Jenny sat back a little on her heels, nodding excitedly. "That's right. I was always a bit mad, you know, and then they sent me here. Nurse says they'll fix me and teach me how to read, so I can take a bit of work in. She said I just have to be a good girl and do as I'm told. Do you think I'm a good girl, Dr Carter? I've been waiting for you."

Rebecca studied her, wondering what to do. The young woman was expectant, waiting for a response, her eyes eager. "I think you're a good girl, Jenny, yes," she murmured, her mind busy. How did she get here? Perhaps it was a dream? She had never really believed in ghosts or the paranormal, but memories of sadness certainly lingered. Was she picking up on something like a memory?

"Is this the hospital, Jenny? Are we in your ward?"

Jenny shook her head, her eyes filling with fear. "Oh, no, Dr Carter, we are not on my ward. I don't want to show you that yet, oh no. I don't want them to see you. Don't let the shadows see you, Dr Carter. They'll call the Shadow Man."

Fear ran through Rebecca's veins. The files referred to the Shadow Man but the shadows, the patient had said that too. Group hallucinations were possible, but from different patients in different years? That was less likely.

"What do you want to show me, Jenny?"

Jenny put her hand out. Rebecca took it gingerly, flinching a little at her cold skin. "I want to show you the garden, Dr Carter. Just follow me, and everything will be alright? Alright? Will you come with me?"

Her sing-song voice was back. Rebecca nodded and stood, brushing her dress off. "I'll come with you, Jenny. Show me your world."

Jenny pulled excitedly, and Rebecca followed, as the walls around her dissolved into dancing white shadows and Jenny hummed her tune, leading her further into the asylum.

Chapter 5
Day 2

"Back to the Archives! That should be a song. It has quite the ring to it." Adam chuckled to himself as he walked, whistling. Rebecca followed in a daze. She didn't know if she felt tired from those strange dreams, or if the overall malaise of the place was getting to her. Everything seemed muffled, the sounds quenched, the colours faded. She kept seeing things out of the corner of her eye, making her jump.

He was talking again. She forced herself to focus and look attentive. "I thought you might want to spend some time on the wards again today, so have arranged a visit with Natalie, you met her yesterday, remember?"

Do you remember me? She shook off the errant thought. "Of course. Which part is she working in?" Her voice sounded a little flat, toneless.

But Adam didn't seem to notice as he rapped out a smart rhythm with his feet, walking along the white corridors quickly. "She's with the older patients to-day, I believe. You should be able to have a nice chat to some of them, they're fairly well behaved. Used to the system, you know."

The system. She imagined lines of patients wrapped in cocoons, kept here for centuries, pressed slowly into the walls. "How long have some of the long-term patients been here?"

Adam paused, eyes narrowing in thought. "Hmm, hmm. I would have to check, and it's not many, mind you, but I think we have a couple of female patients who've been here since they were young. Like eighteen or so. There's nothing much wrong with them, they're just not able to cope outside. In our world, you know."

"Do you know why they were brought here? Or when?"

"Who, the long term ones? Oh, a couple have probably been here sixty years. I bet they could tell some tales!"

Rebecca mused. They probably could. Would they have seen any of the patients from the files, like, Jenny, perhaps? She would have been old, of course, by then, but they might have seen her. *Do you recognise me?* Her echo floated back, caressing Rebecca's ear. Could she find her?

"I think that sounds very good. I would like to speak with some of the long term patients, especially the female patients. Did you know that some of the women who were admitted here weren't even mad, that they were sent here because their parents or husbands decided?"

Adam turned, eyebrows raised. "I did not know that. We have come on some, haven't we! I imagine my wife would love to have me committed sometimes," He winked. "But thankfully, she's not allowed. Can you imagine such a thing!"

Surprisingly, she could. She wondered how many women had been left here to moulder and decay, how many were released, how many were forgotten about.

"Times were different then," she said, quietly. There was nothing else to say. At least now, the hospitals were run properly, with a focus on patient care. The more she studied this area, the more she was grateful that they lived in more enlightened times.

They arrived at the archives door and he turned with a cheerful smile, eager to be off. "Well, here you are, your dusty little corner! I'll be back for you later, alright? And perhaps we could have lunch before I take you to see Natalie?"

His tone was hopeful, a little hesitant. She frowned, but acquiesced, her mind on what lay behind the door. What would she find? Were there details on the experimental treatments? And she really needed to see if she could find out more about Jenny. Would she be there in her dreams if she was released? She doubted it.

"Great," he said, and opened the door for her. It yawned open, exposing lurking shadows, and eerie corners.

"I'll look forward to lunch later. If you find anything interesting, I'll be all ears!"

He giggled as he left, shutting the door with a clang. The key rattled in the lock, before his footsteps marched away. Is that how it felt for the patients, hearing the doors lock behind them? Did they mind? Did they notice, after a while?

She cast a look at the shadows, willing them to stay back, and to not move. But they did not heed her, moving and dancing closer to her, sliding across the floor, pooling like spilled ink at her feet. She took a deep breath, and pulled the files towards her again.

There was no sound but the scratch of her pen and the swish of paper as she pulled them from files, sometimes blowing off the dust that had collected between the pages. Her mind began to tap out the questions, silently, as she read. What was Ward 66? What was the Special Treatment? And who was the Shadow Man? Was he someone? Was he a myth, a boogey man that the patients invented? She did not know, but she suspected they were all linked some-how.

Sighing, she gathered the files up to archive them and pulled open the next drawer. This one was just as full, with neatly stacked fat folders all in a row. She pulled out as many as she could carry, leaving the drawer open. Placing them on the table, she opened the first, and gasped as the pages cut her finger. "Ouch!"

She sucked at the blood, eyeing the tremble in the shadows as they lurched and curled around her in shapes that had nothing to do with the sunlight. These shadows were something else. They were memories, perhaps. And they were waiting for something.

Blotting the blood from her finger against her trousers, she opened the first file, scanning the contents page. This one was mostly expenditure, and salaries of the staff. The esteemed Dr Jonas Floyd was still there, and earning what was probably a very reasonable salary at that point. Her eye caught on another name, one that had been echoing through her mind. Jenny Wilkes, patient orderly. She was still in the hospital then, but earning some kind of money. Had she been released and decided to stay on as an employee? What treatment had she had been given?

She flicked through the other pages, seeing nothing relevant, and then a slip fell from the file, of extra funding arranged for the expansion of the Treatment Centre, headed up by Dr Jonas Floyd. This was something.

She stilled, bringing the pages closer. Silence fell in the room as even the shadow whispers ceased. The hospital had received funding to implement the new reforms that had gained popularity throughout the country, offering a more holistic approach to patient care.

Dr Floyd had access to the latest equipment for his patients, including hydrotherapy procedures and the latest medications to treat disorders such as opium, morphine and mercury. His wards were expanded to incorporate both men and women, treating not only melancholy but also more severe cases such as moral insanity and psychopathy. Dr Floyd's work would be studied and used as examples for teaching. No wonder he had such a good salary. He had become a very powerful man.

There was a newspaper clipping tucked into the file of the good doctor himself opening one of the new wards. He was standing in front of a grand looking building, looking very pleased with himself. He was tall, well-dressed, with cold eyes. She stared at him for a while, before shuddering and tucking the paper away. She didn't want to see that face again. Picking up her pen, she doodled on her paper, writing 66 and drawing black shadows around it, more and more, until it was entirely obscured.

"What did you do to those people, Jonas Floyd?" she whispered. "Am I here to expose you? Did you use your position to become a god within the asylum?" She did not utter her last thought out loud. *Are you the Shadow Man?*

Lunch was surprisingly pleasant. They queued next to staff with IDs and alarms tucked into their belts, who nodded cordially as they waited. The food was local, Adam had explained, as the hospital had kept up the practice of allowing patients to grow produce within the grounds. Taking a quiet table, she began to eat, listening to Adam's gentle chatter.

"And did you make any progress today, Rebecca? Have you found what you were looking for?"

Rebecca paused. Had she found what she was looking for? She grimaced slightly, chewing her food, taking a little extra time. Reaching for her glass of water, she looked at him. The nurse was sitting back in his chair in a show of relaxation, but his eyes were on her face. She wondered how much she should tell him.

"I have found some details, but they are beginning to raise more questions than answers. I've found that Rivers was used as a base for experimental treatments, and there was a lot of research conducted here."

"Experimental? Do you mean like lobotomies?" His excited hiss was loud, causing some of the other diners to look around. He smiled apologetically and leaned closer, lowering his voice. "Do you mean like... the bad stuff?"

"No, not necessarily. They didn't actually perform lobotomies until the 20th century. There is mention of hydrotherapy treatment, which probably was cruel when compared to our modern day standards. It probably was cruel then, too."

Adam frowned, his look of confusion making him look younger. "I thought hydrotherapy was all about steam baths and whirlpools, that sort of thing."

Rebecca nodded. "It is nowadays, and it is certainly therapeutic. But when it was first introduced to treat insanity, they would immerse patients in very hot or very cold baths, or wrap them up in bandages for days at a time. There was quite the scandal in Bedlam when the staff there tortured a patient with water. By the end of the 19th century it was all but obsolete as a practice. But during the time I am researching, it was quite popular. And one of the doctors here at the time, Dr Floyd, was given a lot of funding to do experimental treatments. I'm just not sure what they were yet. Are you familiar with him?"

"Who?"

"Dr Floyd. He was quite an important doctor at the time. I would assume that he's been mentioned in the history at least once."

Adam shrugged in an expansive manner. "Never heard of him, wouldn't want to. I don't think we would have got on!"

He laughed, and Rebecca joined in. "But in all seriousness, Rebecca, this is fascinating. I would love to hear more about it! Perhaps you could show me some of your work this evening, over a drink. Some of us go to the local pub for a few midweek, and you have been working hard, you know."

She smiled absently at his words, noticing his keenness. But she had been working hard, and perhaps a change of scene would help her sleep. It would be nice to see something outside of the hospital. "Sure, why not," she agreed, surprising herself.

Adam beamed, moving a little closer. "Excellent! Now, tell me more about what you've been studying. This is gripping stuff!"

She laughed again, relaxing. Their cups of coffee grew cold as she related tales of the asylums from the nineteenth century, but she did not mention Jenny, or what Annie had said about the shadows. That was not something she wanted to speak about out loud. Not today, not ever.

Chapter 6

After what became an extended lunch, Adam dropped her off at the women's wards, promising to collect her later and show her a good time that evening at the Red Oak. Rebecca realised she was quite looking forward to it.

Natalie was all smiles, introducing her to the patients on the ward, and making sure she was comfortable. This ward was markedly different to the one she had seen just yesterday. There were lines of chairs facing a television that blurted out canned laughter on a daytime TV show. Wrinkled, blank faces were trained on the TV, watching blindly.

The ward smelled clean, but there was a tint of decay to it, much like that of a nursing home. Here, the patients were waiting to die. The thought made her shiver.

She thought about asking what activities they were given to do, like the art classes she had seen in the other ward, but she did not want to seem disapproving or judgmental. Perhaps the older patients didn't want to be kept busy.

Natalie pointed out two women who were sitting away from the television, playing some kind of board game around a small table.

"Those two there will chat to you if you want to do an interview. They've not had their medication yet today, but they're friendly old dears. The one on the left is Harriet and the one on the right is Agatha Rose. They're good friends and do everything together, those two. Why don't you go and get to know them, and I'll pull up the files for the patients here when you're done?"

Rebecca admired Natalie's efficiency and nodded, turning towards the two women. They hadn't noticed her, appearing to be absorbed in their game. She walked over, noting again the quiet, the lack of hushed voices, the absence of spirit. It was as if her own footsteps sank into the floor, silenced, stolen by shadows. She eyed the board as she approached them, not sure what it was they were playing. They still had not acknowledged her. She cleared her throat.

"Um, excuse me, may I join you for a moment? I'm Doctor Carter, Rebecca Carter. I'm spending three days here at the hospital to do research. Would you be willing to speak to me?"

Their faces turned simultaneously, as if one was looking into a mirror and her reflection followed. The one on the left was wrinkled, her hair a little mussed.

But her eyes were bright and astute. The other had an unlined face, with sunken eyes. Her hair was entirely grey, combed into a ponytail. Their expressions were the same, lips slightly parted, eyes wide. At last, the first one took a breath and shook her head.

"Yes, doctor, please sit down. What did you say your name was?"

"Rebecca. Dr Rebecca Carter. And you are?"

I'm called Agatha Rose. I've been here the longest so I take charge of the situations here. This is Harriet, she's a little shy. Say hello, Harriet."

"Hello," Harriet chirped, her mouth moving as if she was a puppet on strings. Her eyes did not leave Rebecca's face.

"Hello, Agatha Rose, Harriet. May I ask, how long have you been here at Rivers?"

Agatha Rose chortled, her hand lifting up to her chest as she laughed, her bosoms shaking. "Oh, Dr Rebecca, you made that sound as if we are here for a week's respite by the sea. That did make me laugh. It was funny, wasn't it, Harriet?"

Harriet paused, then laughed too, a laugh that was the exact copy of Agatha Rose. She stopped suddenly, as if the laugh had fallen from her mouth, or the puppeteer had loosened her strings. Rebecca felt the hairs on the back of her neck rise.

She watched Harriet's eyes, lucid, aware, and afraid. Was she afraid of Agatha Rose, perhaps?

A hand came down on hers, pinning it to the table top, their game forgotten. "Why are you here, Dr Rebecca? What did you seek to find?"

Rebecca started, uncomfortable with the contact and unsure what she was asking. But the woman held strong, her hand clamping hers to the table, holding her in place. "Why are you here, Dr Rebecca?"

Her eyes. There was something about her eyes. It reminded her of so many stories, so many women, who had been sent to these places to be forgotten about. She opened her mouth, then closed it again. "I'm here to find the truth," she replied, simply. Agatha-Rose's grip lessened slightly.

"What have you seen of the place, my girl? Tell me truthfully." Her voice had lowered, so much so that it barely reached Rebecca's ears. She thought for a moment.

"I have been given a tour of some of the wards, and I have seen the Archives."

"And?"

"I have dreamed of the place. I dreamt of a woman from a long time ago."

As Agatha-Rose stared, Harriet sighed, letting out her breath. Sorrow spilled into the old woman's eyes, and she squeezed Rebecca's hand, just once, before releasing her. She picked up her counter again, studying the board. "Your turn, Harriet," she said.

Was that a dismissal? Rebecca wasn't sure. She hesitated, her body braced to leave and move to another table, to build another pointless conversation. But then Harriet turned to her, her eyes serious. "You need to be careful, Dr Rebecca Carter. The shadows are watching you. You can't let the Shadow Man see you. Don't let him."

Rebecca felt a slice of fear moving down her body, numbing her tongue, stilling her movements. "I have heard of the Shadow Man, but I have not found him in the files. Do you see him, Harriet?"

"Shh! Don't speak of him so loud. Don't summon him. This is his place, you know. You have to keep quiet. If he wants you, he'll keep you. Do you want to end up like us?"

Rebecca opened her mouth, and closed it again. What could she say? Not a one of them was here through fault of their own. A diagnosis of mental health was not a blame, a stain on their character. But reminding them that she was not that way, that she was not mentally ill, would set them apart. Put her as something more. She could not do that.

"I will be careful, Harriet," she promised. "I won't let him see me."

Harriet nodded, and her hand slowly extended out, covering her own. But this time it was not to hold her still. It was to give warmth, perhaps. Rebecca turned, looking behind her. She wasn't staff, but she knew that touching patients was a distinct no in this environment. Natalie was standing at the other end of the room, but her eyes were fixed, on her, and her hands. She was watching everything.

Rebecca turned back round, feeling cold. Harriet moved her hands back, and smiled. "Do you play games, Dr Carter?"

The moment had passed. Rebecca declined, moving her chair away and stepping away from the table, walking the room in a leisurely route. Most did not notice her, with their faraway gaze and slack mouth, but one or two patients watched her with guarded eyes. At last she reached Natalie, who was waiting for her. Her face was expressionless, but her mouth was hard. "You really shouldn't let them touch you, you know. I know you don't work here, but. You shouldn't do that."

Rebecca stifled the urge to point out that humans touch, and that it wasn't going to manipulate or condition her into handing over the keys, or turn her into an inmate. Some staff were so conditioned into the idea of them and us that they couldn't see the point. So she said nothing. They stood there in silence for a while, Rebecca thinking about the two women, and what they said. She became aware of the silence, and wondered how she could fill it.

"How long have the women been here on this ward? They seem so, settled, perhaps."

That must have been the cue that Natalie wanted, as she sprang to life, her face animated. "They have been here a long time, as a rule, yes. We do have some older women admitted for a short term but it's fairly unusual. Most are here because they have always been here and now, what would they do? Who would look after them?"

Rebecca looked out on the sea of faces, women who sat there with blank faces, glued to their chairs. Was that what it came to, even now, when institutions prided themselves on care, that some would stay here indefinitely because nobody else cared?

"Is there no programme that integrates them back to the community?"

Natalie scoffed. "Like Probation in the prison estate? That's toothless too. You know, really, that women like this won't return to a happy ever after. Not even now."

Rebecca did know. "And so this is the best that they can hope for?"

Natalie shrugged. "They're well fed, they're safe, they have friends. That's a lot more than some have. We do care for our patients, you know, Rebecca. We know what's best for them."

But do they know? Rebecca doubted that. But perhaps they were safe. She turned away from the women, and then paused, afraid. Someone was humming that tune again, the one she heard Annie hum, and then heard when she was alone. She had just one more day, and then she could leave. She held on to the thought, grasping it as if it were a life raft. Just one more day, Rebecca. One more day.

Chapter 7

"What'll you be having then, Rebecca?"

The pub was busy, with people taking up seats by a roaring fire and eating food at tables. It was a typical pub environment, with an over-patterned carpet, round tables and the ever-present gleaming bar. But it was warm, and noisy, and friendly. She tightened her scarf, feeling the chill that had not left her all afternoon. Adam was waiting, his face expectant. He had put on aftershave, she had noticed. He hoped that he wouldn't get too eager later.

"A white wine for me, please. Dry. Shall I find a table?"

He nodded, disappearing into the crowd purposefully. She skirted the edge of the bodies, tuning into the hum of chatter that was so different from the pace and tone of the hospital. Here it was raucous, animated, and loud. In the hospital it was muted, distant and quiet. Even the hospital staff spoke in fractured sentences, not meaning what they said. This was real. It was a relief to listen to it. It warmed her, almost.

She spotted a table in the corner and made her way to it, settling in with relief. Having a table between them was better than standing, getting buffeted closer by the crowd, creating an enforced, artificial, intimacy. Adam returned quickly, bringing her wine in a large glass and a pint for himself. He beamed as he approached, setting the drinks down.

"You got a table! Well done. So how was your day?"

"Eventful, I suppose. I've not found much more about the treatments yet, but I've got lots of details from the accounts about the kind of work that patients could do while at the hospital, and some even managed to learn a trade while they were here. Certainly it looks like Rivers was run well as an institution, both back then, and now, of course. But I really would like to take a look at some of the old parts of the hospital. I understand that there are some lower floors that have been closed, is that correct?"

Adam took a mouthful of his drink before answering, leaving a film of foam hovering on his top lip. "Yes, that's right, we don't really go there. I don't think there's much to see. What is it that you want to find?"

"I'm not sure. There probably isn't anything, I just want to get a feel for it, maybe. Taking some photographs would be ideal, but I don't have my camera with me and I had to give my phone up, of course."

Adam nodded sympathetically. "The security is tight in Rivers. It's frustrating."

He was frustrating. Rebecca wondered if he would help her. She smiled. "So do you think you could help me?"

"Of course. Help you with what?"

Her lips tightened with annoyance, and she picked up her glass to disguise it. "If you could take me into the old part of the hospital tomorrow. I really want to have a poke around. Will you come with me?"

"Oh, ah, you mean going in there tomorrow! It could be a bit spooky, you know!"

He laughed, his eyes amused. "Sometimes the new ones go in for a dare, but I never have. It's certainly not forbidden, but I would have to request the keys for it. Shall we go together around 10? Would that suit?"

That would do nicely. "Thanks, Adam, I appreciate it. It's not likely I'll find anything, but I do want to see if I can look at some of the Special Treatment Wards."

Adam nodded, thinking. "Are those the wards where he was hosing them down, you said? The insane ones?"

"Right. I doubt the equipment is still there, but sometimes you can get a sense of it, when you're there. You know?"

"I know exactly what you mean. My grandmother's friend used to swear that she could pick things up from objects, details of the past, you know. Sometimes the memories of the past stay with the object or place."

Rebecca was surprised. Perhaps he really did know what she meant. She smiled again, drinking more wine. It really was a pleasant evening, she thought, watching the crowd. She should do this more often instead of being hunched over her computer. Being around people was just necessary, perhaps. She put aside all thoughts of the shadows and the shadow man and enjoyed Adam's attentions instead. She didn't even mind when he ordered more wine and sat just a bit closer. It was fine. She was only here another day.

It was late by the time she managed to return to her room, having had to politely put off an increasingly drunk and hopeful Adam.

She stepped into her room, looking around. Had anything been moved? Had someone been here? She locked the door, then closed the curtains.

She looked around her room again. She was sure something had been moved, something had changed. She shivered.

As she shut her eyes, the whispers began again, gently, as if they were waves crashing against the sea. Quietly, just beyond the shadows, a music box began to play, playing the song that Annie had hummed. Rebecca slept.

Chapter 8

She was back in the asylum.

She recognised the white walls, the crucifix by the door, the big windows that would not open. She went to the door, eager to find Jenny. Would she be somewhere else? Did Jenny call her this time? Or did she call to Jenny? She did not know.

Reaching the corridor, she looked out, wondering if there would be people, if they would see her. Was she a ghost here, perhaps? A dream called from the future, or was she actually here, travelling in time, able to change events? She did not know. The corridor was cool against her feet. She took the left passage, seeing some stairs that led downwards. Was it likely that the main hub of the place was at the bottom, rather than the top?

She reached the stairs, hesitating. Should she go down them? She put her hand on the wall, listening. She could hear no voices, but could feel the thrum of activity. Where were the patients kept? Were they down here? She descended, her eyes searching the gloom. Where were the patients? She passed doorways with rooms just like the one she had found herself in, beds neatly made. She continued, hand on the wall, listening for noise, for a sense of life. There was a passage to the right, but it was dark and hard to see into it. She paused, feeling the urge to go in it, to venture deep into the hospital, to find everything, to uncover its secrets. A whisper unfolded itself from the wall, wrapped in a shadow.

Follow, it breathed. She followed. The passageway was darker, more narrow. She wondered if she was already underground. Blinking, she stepped out into another corridor, almost identical to the one she had been in. She looked left, and right, wondering which way to go. She chose left. The passage was wider. Perhaps it led to somewhere important. She headed down it. The walls were white, just as everywhere else was, but these had a hint of green to them. She looked up, seeing a warm lamp shining above her head. She wondered how it was powered. Had they invented electricity yet? She wasn't sure.

It was so big. It had never felt this big walking the corridors with Adam. Was she in the part that they had closed off? She looked around her again, in interest, noticing the details. She had to be underground here, the passageways were too dark, despite the light and the bland white walls.

She kicked herself for not having a good look out of her window before she started out. But she did not, so now she had to guess.

She continued downwards. The corridor widened, further, and at last she started to see signs for Wards, and offices. Ward 66. Could she perhaps look at it? She might never get the research, but at least if she saw it, with her own eyes, she could get her own answers. She started forward, following the sign for the Wards.

There were no people. Where were the people? There were doors set into the walls but they were closed, with no windows. She wondered if she should look inside, or keep onwards. Something pulled her on. The walls were dark green, with some light seeping in from tiny rectangular windows near the top of the corridor. Here and there were wheelchairs, parked neatly by the walls.

There was another room, this time with double doors and grimy windows. She stepped closer, peering in. The room inside was big, with what looked like dials on the walls. There were six white porcelain bathtubs in a line, covered with some kind of fabric, almost like something you would put on a boat. She pressed her nose up to the glass. Was this a hydrotherapy room?

In the corner, furthest away from the doors she could see a huge circular vat with great bolts in it and pipes connecting to the wall. She puzzled over it.

Could it be the boiler, perhaps? She shivered. Probably best not to know. She stepped away from the window, feeling glad that there was nobody there. She walked hurriedly on, her eyes glancing around to see if she could see signs for the wards. The corridor was wider now, with the walls arching up to the ceiling. In front of her there were great huge wooden doors set into the wall, one after the other. Something told her this was it. It was a ward.

She walked closer, examining the doors to see if there were any numbers on them. She pulled one open gently, setting the door against the wall so it did not bang shut by accident. This may be a dream but she did not want to be trapped.

The ward was a big room lined with beds much like the one she had woken up in, lining each wall. The beds were all neatly made. Here and there were wheelchairs parked, the big iron kind that she had seen in photographs. There were no people. She turned to leave, and paused, her heart beginning to pound.

There was a rocking chair in the corner that started to move, back and forth, by itself. Her eyes were fixed on the sight of the empty chair, rocking. The fear pooled in her limbs, and she could not move. The chair began to move faster and the whispers returned, as the shadows began to slide down the walls from the ceiling. She did not like this at all. Gasping, she ran out of the ward, hastily shutting the door behind her.

She ran right into Jenny.

Rebecca's scream rang out, echoing and bouncing in the huge space, then falling at her feet. Jenny was motionless, staring at her with wide eyes.

At last, she spoke. "What are you doing here, Dr Carter? How did you get here?"

Rebecca blinked, recovering herself. "I don't know, I woke up here. Did you not call me?"

Jenny shook her head slowly.

"But if you did not, who did?"

Jenny did not answer, but instead she looked up and around, her eyes fearful. "Come on," she whispered. "Lets get you somewhere safer."

She pulled on her arm, then started to walk down the corridor. Rebecca hesitated. "Will you show me Ward 66, Jenny?"

Jenny looked back, her eyes shocked. "Where did you hear about that? No, I'm not showing you that. Come on!"

Rebecca stayed still, her feet rooted to the ground. "I really need to see it, Jenny. Will you show me the treatment rooms?"

Jenny shook her head. "You don't know what you're asking me, Dr Carter. Don't ask that of me. I don't want to go back there."

Her voice wobbled, betraying her fear, her pain. Rebecca felt a stab of guilt. She was so wrapped up in her need to see that she had forgotten that Jenny had experienced it here. "I'm sorry, Jenny. We can go. But

53

I haven't seen anyone, you know. I don't think there's a danger of the shadows today."

Jenny gave her a strange look again but did not reply, instead taking her arm and walking her down the corridor. Rebecca looked at her, wondering what was different. She looked a little older, and she had lost that singsong way of speaking that she had last time. Had it been so long?

"Do you know what year it is, Jenny?"

Jenny scrunched her face up, clearly thinking, but did not slow her stride. They passed doors on either side, Jenny's feet marching out a quiet beat as they walked.

"I don't know, Miss. It's difficult to say, really. We're just here. We've always been here. You called me here so it must be a time that you know, but I don't know myself when it is. It just is."

Rebecca pondered her statement. "What do you mean by we, Jenny? The hospital is empty except for me and you."

Jenny gave her a strange look again, and then her gaze skittered to the walls. "No, Miss. It's just you don't see them."

"See who?"

"Them. The people in the walls. You don't see them."

Rebecca felt a chill again, recalling the rocking chair, and the shadows. "I don't see who, Jenny?"

"The shadow people. Like me. Like you. We've always been here, don't you see?"

Rebecca frowned, slowing her steps. "You've always been here, Jenny. But I haven't. I've only been here two days. Don't you remember?"

Jenny wouldn't meet her gaze. "I wouldn't know about that, Miss. But if you look, you'll see them. They're there."

Her eyes swept the corridor, over the walls, the floors. It felt like she was trying to manhandle an imaginary friend, to appease a small child.

"Alright, Jenny. Have it your way. Where are you taking me?"

Jenny pulled on her hand again. "I'm taking you to where it's safe, Miss. Come on. Walk faster, before they hear you."

That did it. She walked faster, resisting the urge to hold Jenny's hand. But the fear lodged itself in her throat, crouching there, making it hard to swallow. Doors whistled past, one after the other. Jenny at last paused, pulling on a door and gesturing for her to step inside.

"Come on," she whispered. "We'll be safe here. This is where I stayed."

It was a ward like the other one, with rows of black metal beds, one after the other. There was nothing on the beds, no personal effects, or books, or photographs. Rebecca wondered if they were allowed anything like that.

"Which one is your bed, Jenny?"

Jenny gave her that strange look again, as if she were eyeing a wild animal that might bite at any moment. She pointed, her hand shaking ever so slightly. "That one."

She pointed to a bed at the end, a bed like all the others. Rebecca eyed it then looked back, confused. Why was she so afraid? What was she looking at?

She followed Jenny's gaze back to the bed. It was still empty. And then slowly, the bed began to change, shimmering, fading in and out, like a flicker on an old black and white tv. There was something over the bed. Was it a curtain, perhaps?

She stepped closer then stopped, the horror bringing bile up into her throat. She covered her mouth with her hands. There was a shape hanging over the bed, face thankfully obscured by the long dark hair. Obscured by Jenny's hair. Jenny had hanged herself above her own bed. She was dead.

Chapter 9
Day 3

It felt like ten am would never arrive. Rebecca waited around in the conference room as she was unable to find another escort to the archives, and Adam was nowhere to be seen. He was either hungover or getting the keys for the old part of the hospital, she supposed.

She had seen Dr Julian briefly on the way to the conference room, and he promised to check in with her later about her findings.

She did not mention that she had found hardly anything concrete on what actual treatments the hospital had used. She imagined writing down her dreams in her research paper, and handing that to her editor. She would be laughed out of town. Or put somewhere like here! She shivered.

That was not a funny thought.

The image of Jenny's hanging dead body flashed up in her mind and her stomach lurched again. What could have caused her to hang herself? When did she do it? If the files were kept accurately, then she had been given the job of orderly perhaps five years after she had been admitted. Did it make her unhappy? Did she die young? Or as a middle-aged woman, realising that was all her life had left? She did not know.

Her finger started to hurt and she looked at it, confused. She had chewed the nail down to the quick, leaving it raw and bleeding. When had she done that? She did not remember.

She took her notes out, spreading them in front of her. She really needed more proof to link up the experimental treatments with the mysterious Dr Floyd. Perhaps she should do one more trip to the Archive this afternoon before the car came to collect her this evening. She stretched, feeling her bones pop. Tonight she could sleep in her own bed and start to write up the notes on her computer. She could check back in with emails and text messages, and reintegrate herself with life again. She could close the Rivers chapter for good. Nodding, she arranged the papers in a pile. One more day.

Out of the corner of her eye, she saw movement, a flash of black. She stilled, turning her head, as her heart started to pound. What was that? The conference room was light and shadow free. Nothing moved. Her eye fell on the photographs, glass gleaming in the sun. There was one frame on the wall, there was something familiar about it.

She pushed away from the desk, walking over. The photograph gazed back at her, witnessing her expression in the glass as her mouth went slack. The man. It was him. Dr Floyd. He was standing in front of the asylum, face impassive.

She stepped back, shivering. Of course he was in this picture. He was an influential member of the team, and he brought in a lot of research funding. It didn't mean anything. She looked again at the photo, arms folded across her chest. It was so cold in here all of a sudden. She blinked. For a moment, it almost looked like he was looking directly at her. And he was smiling.

The door opened and Adam walked in, his face triumphant, holding up an old looking set of keys. "Guess who's going ghost hunting, baby!"

Still rattled, Rebecca ignored the obnoxious comment, moving back around the table. "That's great. I'm excited to see it, shall we go now?"

Adam looked surprised. "Of course, if you're so keen to get in there, lets do it. If you get scared you can always hold my hand, you know!"

Rebecca smiled a thin smile back. Perhaps reminding him that he had a wife would not be the best response when she wanted to go and see the old part of the hospital, and they would not give her the keys so she could go by herself. But she didn't know how long she could take of his awkward flirting. It was a shame she couldn't offer him up to the Shadow Man.

She laughed to herself, then shivered. Maybe not even that.

The nurse coughed awkwardly and cleared his throat. "Alright, do you need to bring anything with you? I suggest you wear comfortable shoes, it might be a bit uneven underfoot here and there. Oh and a jacket, maybe. It's underground so will probably be cold."

That was a good idea. She agreed, lifting her jacket from the back of the chair and heading out, keeping her eyes far away from that particular photograph. It was just her imagination overreacting, of course. But just in case, she wasn't looking again. As she stepped through the door, the whispers started again.

This time they took a different route through the hospital, having their faces confirmed before the doors opened, and locking and unlocking endless doors. The clash and click lingered in Rebecca's ears like an angry tinnitus. Adam didn't seem to mind it.

This part of the hospital was more faded, and not as cheerful. The shadows followed, sliding along the floor, flirting with Adam's steps as he marched forward. It was cold.

At last they reached a part of the building that had older stonework, and some scaffolding left behind, tucked behind staircases and lying next to doors. Adam stopped at a door that was set into a large piece of wood and began to rummage through the keys. "It's one of these ones. Hang on, he did tell me which. Hang on," he murmured, as he picked one up, discarded it, and found another on the ring. "Ah here it is. He said it would stand out. Lets do this then."

He paused, turning, the keys dangling in his hand. "If you're sure? It's not too late to back out, you know."

"Open it up, Adam."

His face faltered. "Alright, alright, no need to be so serious about it. It was just a joke. Come on then, lets go see what there is!"

The door creaked open, and they stepped into the old part of the asylum.

Clang. The key locked them inside, and the echo rose to the ceiling. Rebecca stood there, looking around, and feeling the atmosphere. This was it. This was where she had been, or one part of it. Somewhere in here lay her answers. She knew it.

"Well, this is a bit creepy, isn't it! I mean, it's not like the Youtube videos you see where there's trolleys lying around, and empty beds, but there's something funny about it. It makes my hair stand up."

"There's lots of memories in here. Lots of misery, too. It's bound to affect the place. Look, that corridor there looks like a main one. I suggest we follow it and look for signs for the wards. Alright?"

"Alright," Adam muttered sulkily as he followed. "I didn't know you had a map of the place, it sounds like you're familiar with it!"

"I've studied lots of floor plans of old asylums. Perhaps something just rubbed off?"

Adam was not convinced, but he caught up with her, fumbling with his torch. "I thought of these, they might be useful. Especially if we have to go further underground."

Rebecca took the spare from him gratefully. That was something she had not thought of. She switched it on, seeing dust lift from the floor. The place was empty. Not even a rat ran past. "So why have you never been in here then? You mentioned last night, that the new ones come in for a dare but you never have."

Adam fidgeted a bit, then mumbled, "Well, it's not that I'm scared, or anything, but I'm a bit superstitious, maybe. I'd rather let sleeping dogs lie, if you will."

Rebecca laughed. Her laugh fractured and lifted, the echo bouncing up and down again. "Well we shan't break anything. I just want to have a look and then we can go back."

He looked visibly relieved. She stifled the urge to laugh again.

Their footsteps were swallowed up by the dust, muffled. It was as if they were walking on clouds, silently. The corridors were wide and smooth, and quiet. Rebecca saw no shadows, heard no whispers. They reached a crossroads, the four different corridors going off in different directions.

"Where now, then?" Adam asked, waving his torch back and forth. Rebecca stepped forward, looking on the walls for signs. There were none.

"I'm not sure. I think if we take that corridor there, which goes downwards, we should reach the wards. Shall we?"

Adam trundled off, shaking his head, his torch light wobbling back and forth. Rebecca started walking, feeling faint strains of familiarity about the place. "Look, those doors look like the ward doors, I think we're getting close!"

He raised his eyebrows, eyeing the doors. "These are like the ward doors? How did they see in to check on the patients?"

"I don't think they did. There were a few cases of fires in asylums where lots of patients died, as they couldn't get out. All the doors were locked."

"Really? That's barbaric!"

"It was. Scandals like that reached the press, eventually, and after a while the reformers got involved. Things got better, for a time. Then they got worse again."

Rebecca's torch beam caught on something and she darted forward to investigate it. In the rubble that had collected at the edge by the wall, there was a partially submerged doll, one blue eye gleaming. She pulled it out, wiping its face, stroking its cheek. Who did it belong to? Did a child from the asylum love this doll? Was it precious to someone?

Adam came up behind her. "What did you find, then?"

She showed him the grimy doll, watching him recoil. "Oh that's terrifying! I hadn't expected to see one of those in here. Put it back, quickly! You don't know where it's been!"

Rebecca laughed, but put the doll down, carefully. It had been loved by someone. She was almost sure of it. She started to hum to the doll, stroking its face, saying farewell. As she straightened, Adam gave her a curious look but he said nothing.

"Come on," he said. "Lets find these wards for you and get back. This place is beginning to give me the creeps."

She agreed, her eyes darting about. Would they have kept the equipment that she had seen? That would be something. If that was the case, the hospital management could even set up a museum in the grounds, perhaps, or just outside. Something to preserve the history of the place.

There were doors on either side now, great polished slabs of wood that lined the walls. Rebecca felt a shiver of excitement. This was the place, she knew it. This was where she had met Jenny. "Here we are," she said, pointing to the doors. "Let's have a look inside. I want to see if anyone left anything."

Adam was sweating, the tang of his fear palpable. But he swallowed nervously and nodded, opening the door to the ward nearest to them. The door creaked. It was loud.

The ward was dark and heavy with a sense of waiting. She raised the torch, seeing lines of black bedframes, some still flush against the wall, some askew. There was rubble, debris strewn everywhere. It crunched underfoot. Rebecca noticed something on the wall next to a bed, and she stepped closer to investigate it. Marks had been scratched into the wall but she couldn't make it out.

"Adam, come and have a look at this, I think it's writing. Can you make it out?"

Adam's voice quivered. "If you don't mind, Rebecca, I'm going to stay right here by the door. I don't like this place one bit. Can you, you know, hurry it along a little?"

She ignored him. There was nothing to fear here. Not for her, anyway. She knew this place. She stepped around beds, moving towards the corner, wondering if there would be something left there, something left by Jenny. A keepsake, perhaps, or even a letter. She knew there was something there. There had to be.

The bed, there in the corner, pulled her closer, as if it was a current. Her feet kept stepping forward, her eyes wide. "Jenny," she whispered. "Jenny."

Nobody answered. The room got darker. Adam called out something but it was indistinct, faint. The room rippled and shifted, and there she was, Jenny, hanging again from the ceiling, dark hair forward, face obscured. She was so close to her.

"Look, she's here!" she called out to Adam, pointing. "This is how some of them ended up. Isn't it tragic?"

Adam didn't answer. Rebecca touched Jenny's foot, reverently. Her bed was still made, the crisp white cotton tucked in neatly at each corner. She noticed something lying against the pillow and she reached out to take it. It was a small leather book, still warm to the touch. She knew it.

Jenny had left her record behind, so she could be remembered. She tucked it into her pocket quickly, breathing her thanks to Jenny. She turned back, seeing Adam framed in the doorway, his face white.

"Seriously, Rebecca, we need to go. We've been here ages and you've just been standing there. Did you not hear me? I really want to go."

Rebecca blinked, confused. "Of course. I only wanted to see the place and get an idea of its ambience. Lets go back. Can you drop me back off at the Archives? I want to double check a few things."

Adam sighed with relief as she stepped out of the room, shutting the door behind him. "You're not finished with Ward 66, then? You're a determined one. I bet your research project is going to be fascinating when it's done. Can we have a copy when it's published?"

Rebecca smiled gaily at him. "Of course! You can all have a copy. And I will mention you in the acknowledgments for all the help you've given me too. You've been a champ!"

Adam looked a lot less afraid now they were leaving the old part of the building, but he kept sneaking glances over his shoulder and shivering. "It's cold in here. I'll drop you off at the Archive and then take the keys back. When do you want picking up?"

She thought for a moment. Around two would be fine. I have time to do a debrief with Dr Julian and then arrange my files before my taxi comes for me."

Adam smiled sadly. "And that's the end of our adventure then? Everything goes back to normal?"

"Exactly. Everything is back to normal."

He nodded, fidgeting with the keys. "Back to normal. After that experience, I can live with it!"

Rebecca laughed again. This time she fancied that she heard the echoes of another laughing with her, a young voice that faded back into the walls almost as soon as she heard it. She smiled.

Chapter 10

The Archives welcomed her like an old friend, with the dusty filing cabinet and the shadows coiling around her feet as she walked. Adam hadn't lingered, still looking worse for wear after his adventure. She sat down at the table, pushing aside the files, and opened the book.

> Dear Diary. Or Book, I suppose. A nurse gave me this when we were finishing our chores and said I could practice my writing in it. It was very kind of her. Normally I only practice when I have to write bills for Cook. My name is Jenny Wilkes and this is my story. I don't suppose it's a very interesting story, but it is my story and I will tell it. I am 25 years old and I have been an inmate at Rivers Asylum since I was 17 years old. I know I will never be released, even though my treatments are

done with. They said there's nobody out there to look after me, so it's better for me to stay here. I don't know about that, I'm sure I could find a spot of work somewhere, but they're the doctors and nurses and they probably know best. I wouldn't know where to start anyway. I'm used to this place.

Rebecca paused, her fingers tracing the handwriting, the lines in the book. This was an invaluable find. How many inmates could even read or write? Or had access to writing materials, for that matter? This was something she could use in her research, something never seen before. The hospital may want it back after, of course, but this would add so much flavour to her research.

"Thank you, Jenny," she whispered.

She flipped forwards a couple of pages, scanning the words.

Today I was asked to help do the intake for the new patients for Special Treatment. Nurse Proctor was there and said that I'd grown up into a fine young woman. She is still scary looking, with that hungry look in her eye. She looked excited when the new patients came in. I think she enjoys her work too much. The tall doctor was there, too, the one with the beard and the smart coat. He didn't look at us, of course. We're just his pets. He tests us and makes notes and sends them to his fancy doctor friends. They weren't there today. When they come, we have more volunteers for special treatment so they can all have a go. If you're a trusted patient, like me, you don't have to do it, but they give you extra treats if you do. Sometimes I think about it, about whether I could do it for a new dress or something. But I don't think I could ever set foot on that ward again.

She shut the book with a snap. This was the key, the evidence that she needed. Treating them like pets, the doctors from London, probably, coming down and experimenting on the patients. As if they were animals! She took a deep breath and opened the book again. Would she tell her more about Ward 66?

They took the new ones to Special Treatment. I don't know what they did but I think they all got the water. They were screaming a lot. It's so noisy at night, and you get used to it, but then when they do the baths, the screaming is even louder. I

don't blame them. It feels like you're being buried alive, wrapped in that shroud
and stuck in a freezing cold bath. And
then they let the water drip on you while
you can hardly breathe in there. I don't
see how it helps my insanity go away,
when I'm screaming like a wild animal in
a bathtub. But they seem to like it. They
write a lot about it and keep doing it even
though they must know all about it by
now.

Rebecca realised she was crying, crying for women
and men who had died so long ago. Being buried alive.
This was barbaric.

It's a bad day today. I had been quite keen
on one of the fellows here, not that he
spoke to me much, they keep us sepa-
rate, you know. But he looks sick. They've
moved him to the sanatorium and put him
on isolation just in case it's something
infectious. I would have liked to tell him
before he went. I don't suppose I'll see
him again. He looked like an old man,
withered and bent. We don't last long in
this place. I'm telling you, diary, because
I can't show it here. If anyone thinks I've

got the purple, they'll give me medicine again. I don't want that medicine. I don't know what they did to me that time but I remember my jaw hurt as if I had been chewing on a bit of wood for a week. I came round with a head full of porridge and pains all over my body. They had me for two days in there. Maybe they gave me the twilight sleep. I'll have to be normal, and not show any lustful urges. It's wanton, for a woman like me. Nurse Proctor would strike that sin right out of me.

Rebecca realised she was staring into space, hot tears rolling down her cheeks. This was a find, of course, and it was a great boon for her research, but this was also an account of how patients were treated, then. Thank God it wasn't the case now. She would have to show this to Dr Julian and ask permission to take it with her. She collected the files that she had put aside to copy, and put the rest neatly back into the filing cabinet. Casting one final look around the room, she whispered a farewell to the shadows that curled and looped around the edges. "May you all be at peace, now. I'll not forget you. I'll write about you."

As she turned to leave, opening the door, the shadows converged, snaking together, drawing up into a shape on the wall. A man stood there in a hat and coat.

His nose was sharp and he had a beard. His eyes were dark holes that watched her as she left.

The corridors all looked the same, with their green linoleum floors and plain walls stretching into the distance. Which way was it back to the conference rooms? She was sure she could make it back, and speak to Dr Julian right away. It would be fine. She held her files carefully, clutching them to her chest, and set off, hoping she was going in the right direction. Her feet slapped against the floor, leaving an echo behind. It was so dark. Perhaps it was going to storm. She reached the end of the corridor and paused, unsure of which way to go. An orderly was walking towards her, whistling.

"Excuse me," she called. He paused. "Can you direct me to the conference rooms or Dr Julian's office? I've been in the Archives and I think I took the wrong turning, somewhere."

He smiled, assessing her face. Rebecca wished that she had wiped the tears from her face or at least checked to make sure her makeup hadn't run. She probably looked a bit dishevelled. But he nodded, pointing towards another corridor and walked with her. "So you're a doctor here, are you, madam?"

"Kind of. I am a doctor, but I don't work here. I've been doing research here, for the last three days. I'm finishing today, though."

"Very good," he replied. "I can take you to the first set of doors ahead, and they'll buzz you through. Have you got your ID handy?"

Her ID? Confused, she looked for her bag. "My ID? Do you mean my driving licence or something? I had to leave all that outside."

The orderly shook his head. "No, love, I mean the ID they gave you when you came in. Do you have it?"

Oh the piece of plastic that they put her photograph on. She reached for her belt, fingers searching for the cord that it was attached to. There was no cord. His eyes followed hers then travelled back up to her face.

"Oh, I don't seem to have it. We, Adam and I, we were investigating the old asylum this morning. I must have dropped it. Will it be a problem?"

"No, it should be fine. They have a record of your face, right?"

Right. She nodded, relieved. He nodded too, picking up his pace.

They reached the doors, plain wooden doors with reinforced glass in. The camera winked on and waited. The orderly waved. Rebecca clambered closer, remembering that she had to be close for them to see her. Nothing happened. The red light went out.

She put her hand on the door handle, expecting to feel the buzz reverberate through her hand. Nothing happened. The orderly huffed out through his nose.

"What's happening?" Rachel asked. "Why aren't they buzzing me through?"

The orderly shrugged. "Maybe they need to see your ID. Sometimes they're strict like that. It's no problem. I'll take you back to the main ward and the nurses can call for your Andrew, alright?"

He wasn't hers, and he wasn't an Andrew. But he was being kind, so it would be rude to correct him. With one hopeful glance back at the camera, she walked back into the asylum with the orderly.

Chapter 11

She was so confused. The lights kept flickering, and faces kept moving in and out in slow motion. Her lips were dry. She tried to wet them, but her tongue felt out of place, huge, in her mouth. "Water, please" she gasped. Silence.

Where was she? She was in bed. Was she tired? She tried to lift her arm. It wouldn't move. Had she been in a fall? What happened?

Her brain

Dissociation

DSM 5 DSM 5 Dissociation

She was in the lecture theatre, sitting next to that cute student, watching the lecturer speak at the front.

"DSM-5. Dissociation. Amnesia, depersonalisation, problems deep in the brain." He stared right at her, and winked.

"Shadow shadow shadow Becca. Yeah."

Blink blink blink

What happened

What happened

To me

Her eyes screeched open. The light was above her, shining. Heads loomed, dancing, mouths leering.

"What is your name?"

"I'm Rebecca. Dr Rebecca. I -"

They were gone. She blinked. It was dark. Where was she? She couldn't move. Cord wrapped around her wrist. She moved her wrists, feeling the restraints, her arms feeling the sheets underneath. Why was she restrained? What had happened?

She shook her head, concentrating. She went to the ward with, who? The orderly. The orderly. They were going to help her find Andrew. No. Not Andrew. Who? Dr Dr Dr who?

The thought flitted away. Her head was spinning. Where was she?

She strained her neck to the right. She was in a room, a room with smooth white walls. She peered,

looking for her arms, seeing them pinned to something with restraints. She was

Kidnapped
That makes no sense
I was
Doing research
I was
Why am I here

Her eyes opened. Everything was moving, switching
back and forth like an old movie. The room shook,
switching frame by frame. She blinked, feeling dizzy.
Nauseous.

She concentrated on white walls. No, green walls.
Green walls.

A face slid into her vision, and she saw red curls
beneath a white cap. Her eyes were
No
Her eyes were
Laughing
No
Her face was laughing
Eyes excited
Sweaty hands pressing down

"Don't you worry, dear. Nurse Proctor will make it go away. I'll make it go all away."

She licked her lips. Sunlight streamed in through windows at the top, tiny rectangular windows. Her legs were encased, her body wrapped in linen. She could not move. She moved her head, from side to side.

A face appeared, hand stroking the face. Her face. Stroking HER face.

"Don't worry, dear, it will be fine. We will look after you. We will look after you."

She opened her mouth to ask who they were, and where she was, but she could not speak, her mouth was covered by linen, and her eyes, her eyes, she could not see. Her body plunged into freezing cold water, and her mouth stretched wide, ripping, open.

Wild animals in a grave. NO. Wild animals in a bathtub. Who said that? Who

WHO

Reality snaps

Standing in the ward and watching the staff watching a woman who looks as if she has been attacked. She is shrieking.

So loud it hurts it's so loud why is she shrieking

Her ID has been taken, she is a doctor. *So aggressive. Not a doctor.* She holds papers like they are a new-born and flinches when someone tries to take them. Her face is dirty. *Not a doctor.*

The nurses shake their heads, giving each other looks. They don't believe her. Nobody believes her. *Not a doctor.*

She puts her hand on the desk – *so aggressive* – and asks for a man to come and get her. She gives a name. Dr Rebecca Carter. The nurses nod and call, and then they put the phone down and shake their head.

"Dr Carter has already left the building. I'm sorry."

She keens, head back, mouth open, as if she is a wild animal. The nurses look, again, and nod. One inches away. They're getting the sleep stuff.

I watch her, the woman, watch her come undone, her mouth unravelling, her howl, unstitching her from the inside.

The nurses watch her, seeing her scream. They come back, hand hiding the sleep stuff, grabbing her elbow. It's done in a flash. She screams, her mouth hollow, as she thrashes, and collapses.

The nurse turns.

"It's alright. It's alright. We will look after her. It's alright. She's just a bit upset. It's alright."

Light climbed in, fighting through the cloth. She was mummified. How long had she been here? Her brain felt clear, connected. She moved her nose, feeling the cotton. It smelled familiar. She breathed it in. She knew that smell.

It was so quiet, still. Where was she?

Whispers floated closer, holding her still.

She lay still, feeling nothing but the cloth. Seeing nothing but the light. Hearing nothing but the whispers. She was here. That was all.

That was all.

She was awake. The room was still. Her brain was clear. She was here.

A door opened, CLACK she knew that sound

Someone

Kneeled down in front of her. She examined his face. His eyes were kind, his mouth was soft. "We are trying to help you. Please let us help you. Tell us your real name. We know you are not Dr Carter. What is your name?

She did not have a name. Who was she?

NOT Dr Carter

NOT

She stared into his eyes. So soft.

"Please tell us your real name. We want to help you."

"I don't know. Not Dr Carter."

He smiled, eyes softening. "That's right. You're doing so well. Not Dr Carter. Well done."

She had pleased him. A rush of feeling ran through her body. She did well.

"What can I call you? I need a name."

He needs a name. He needs a name. She looked around, eyes dazzled by the white.

"Will you look after me?"

He nodded. "We will look after you. Just give me a name. So we can help you."

Just a name. It was just a name. To please him.

NOT Dr Carter. It makes them angry.

"Maybe, Jenny?"

His beam leapt from his face, blazing approval. "Oh such a beautiful name. Well done, Jenny. I am so proud of you!"

She beamed, laughing, basking. "Jenny. Jenny. Jenny."

He smiled again. "Hello Jenny. Don't worry. Everything will be just fine."

About the Author

Eryn was born and raised in Oxford, UK but nowadays lives in South Germany with their young family. They want to travel the world and visit all the mountains, lakes and of course vineyards. When they are not dreaming of travel or writing poetry, they work as a freelance English teacher.

Eryn is a poet and an accidental novelist. They studied Poetry and Playwriting at University but never actually intended to write fiction at all. That changed sometime in 2021 when they began to write flash fiction, which then grew into short stories, and then a couple of those stories developed into ideas for a novel.

Their writing largely leans to the dystopian and the supernatural, depending on which genre they write in. They are currently working on a horror about a sentient and feral bookshop, continuing the dystopian Sci-Fi series based in Woestynn, and working on Book 2 of The Sovereigns.

Eryn is at present obsessed with cheese, dragons, brown noise and strange esoteric videos on Youtube that make you sound like you are sitting in a bomber plane. When not writing you can find them on Blue Sky or Tiktok, generally spreading upheaval of some kind or another.

www.ingramcontent.com/pod-product-compliance
Ingram Content Group UK Ltd.
Pitfield, Milton Keynes, MK11 3LW, UK
UKHW011935190925
7985UKWH00017BA/89